Painting Everything in the World
Copyright ©2018 Tara Books Pvt. Ltd.
For the illustrations: Harsingh Hamir
For the text: Gita Wolf

For this edition:
Tara Books Pvt. Ltd., India, tarabooks.com
and Tara Publishing Ltd., tarabooks.com/uk

Design: Jonathan Yamakami
Cover Design: Dhwani Shah
Production: C. Arumugam
Printed in India by Canara Traders and Printers, Chennai

ISBN: 978-93-83145-48-5

Painting Everything in the World

Harsingh Hamir & Gita Wolf

This is the story of a Rathwa village. It is morning, and people are up early, going about their chores.

A cat spots a snake and jumps up on the roof.

**"What!
Six o'clock already?"**
A man says, hurrying
off to chop firewood.

A few men have set off into the forest, they're looking for small animals to hunt.

A drummer goes along behind them, scaring off the tigers and big cats.

Dhum!   **Dhum!**

Dhum!

A huge feast has been planned in the village, for the Holi festival. Everyone is busy and happy, cleaning, cooking and preparing for the night.

**"It's all ready, I don't think
we've forgotten anything!"**
People say to each other.

"Here! Come back with that broom!" Two men shout at a boy.

Some people are really in a hurry, and start eating and drinking even before everything is ready. There's mahua to drink, and a huge meal of rice, dal, and chicken.

It's a fine night.

"The moon's up!"
Someone calls, looking
out of his hut.

"It's time!"

Men and women make a circle, drummers and
musicians in the middle, and swing into a dance.

A peacock joins in.

It's the best Holi celebration the village has had,
as long as people can remember.

But the next day, something strange happens. All the animals look scared. Everything seems to be going wrong.

"There's no water to cook with!"
Women tell each other.

"This cow has no milk!"
The milkman cries.

**"There's no water
in the wells!"**

"Our baby is sick!"
A woman cries to her husband.

As time goes on, things only get worse.
People wail and cry, day after day.

"Ooh my stomach!"
A man moans, lying on his bed.

"The fields are dry!"

**"There's nothing for
the animals to eat!"**

"The trees are bare!"   "My buffalo is dead!"

"What's going on?"
People ask each other.

"What shall we do now?"
Nobody is sure, but they
all know that things can't
go on like this.

"Let's go ask the Wise Man!"
Someone suggests finally.
"He's sure to know what to do!"

So they go to the Wise Man and say:
**"Why is this happening to us?
We worked hard, we looked after
our fields and animals, we cleaned
our houses, we celebrated Holi…"**

**"Haven't you
forgotten something?"**
The Wise Man asks.

**"What about honouring our
gods, Pithora and Pithori?
Did the artists make
a Pithora painting?"**

**"Oh no, we forgot
to paint our gods!"**
The artists of
the village cry.

It's true. The village wall with the Pithora painting is broken, and the paint is peeling off.

"No wonder!"
People say to each other.

"We've been too busy to think about Pithora!"

"Let's get to work!"
The artists decide.

**"It's time to invite good
fortune back to the village."**
The birds and animals
look relieved.

A Pithora painting must be completed in one night,
so all the people of the village come to help the artists.
"How about some music?" asks a man carrying a drum.

The Wise Man comes too, and tells the artists what to paint. **"Don't leave out anything!"** he reminds them. **"Make sure you show everything in the world!"**

By morning,
it's ready!

"We honour you!"
People pray to the painting.
"Send us good fortune!"

It shows everything in the world: the sun and the moon,
good spirits and evil ones, all kinds of animals and plants,
people working and having fun... the artists are satisfied.

It's a beautiful Pithora painting, showing the gods Pithora and Pithori in the form of horses, along with all the other gods and goddesses.

Everyone is overjoyed. Musicians take out a big procession through the village, and the drummer is in front chanting.

"Good fortune!
Good fortune to everyone!"

"For me too!"
A small boy says.

Pithora Painting

HARSINGH HAMIR, the artist who created the images for this book, is a *lakhara*—or painter—from the Rathwa tribe in Gujarat.

Traditionally each year, a group of such artists is invited by members of the Rathwa community to paint a ritual wall mural called 'Pithora'. The painting is believed to remove ill-luck and restore peace and prosperity to the household which commissions it. Pithora murals are not merely decorative: they capture the whole body of myth, belief and ritual of the community, passed on from generation to generation. A typical Pithora painting honours the gods Pithora and Pithori, depicted in the form of horses. They are shown in the centre row, flanked by the horses of Rathwa ancestors. The top part of the painting generally represents the world of the gods, along with the sun and the moon. The lower half depicts the myth of creation, showing the earth, the farmer, the cowherd, the kings, the trader, the shaman, the goddesses of destiny, the cow, the bull, and various creatures of the forest. A Pithora mural is not yet done when the artists finish painting: to be complete, it needs to be part of an elaborate ceremony in which a *badva*—shaman or healer—performs the rites of 'reading' and interpreting the painting to the assembled members of the community. A large and happy communal feast then follows, which includes performances by musicians and dancers.

Pithora wall mural commissioned by The Museum of Mankind, Bhopal

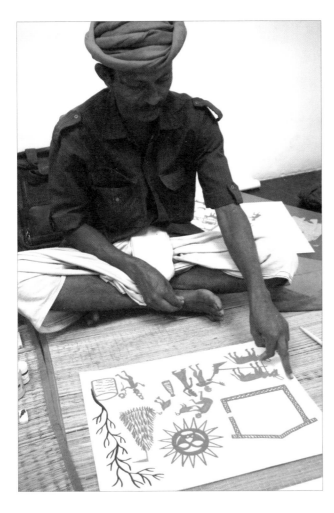

Harsingh Hamir

While this traditional practice continues to this day, several contemporary Rathwa artists have taken new directions which give them additional sources of income. Ranging from wall murals to paintings on canvas and other material, they have begun creating Pithora paintings simply as art which is exhibited and sold in museums, galleries or craft bazaars. While the artists are proud of their heritage, they are very clear, though, that these 'secular' paintings are not to be confused with the ones created in a traditional ritual context.

Harsingh Hamir is one such artist, happy to apply his skills and talent to new material. When we suggested that we make a book together which re-creates the myth of how the Pithora painting came to be, he was delighted with the project. From his oral narrative, and with the aid of contemporary design, we put together a story on how and why the painting is made—which not only showcases a wonderful Pithora painting, but also restores the art to its context in a way only a book is able to do.